The El and the Six Wise Men

A traditional tale from India retold by Alan Trussell-Cullen

Illustrations by Luke Jurevicius and Toby Quarnby

Chapter 1

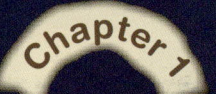

The Six Wisest Men in the Whole World

Many years ago in a town in India, there were six men who were sure they were very wise. In fact they called themselves the Six Wisest Men in the Whole World!

They had spent their whole life gazing up at the stars and the moon and even the sun – because they thought that would make them wise.

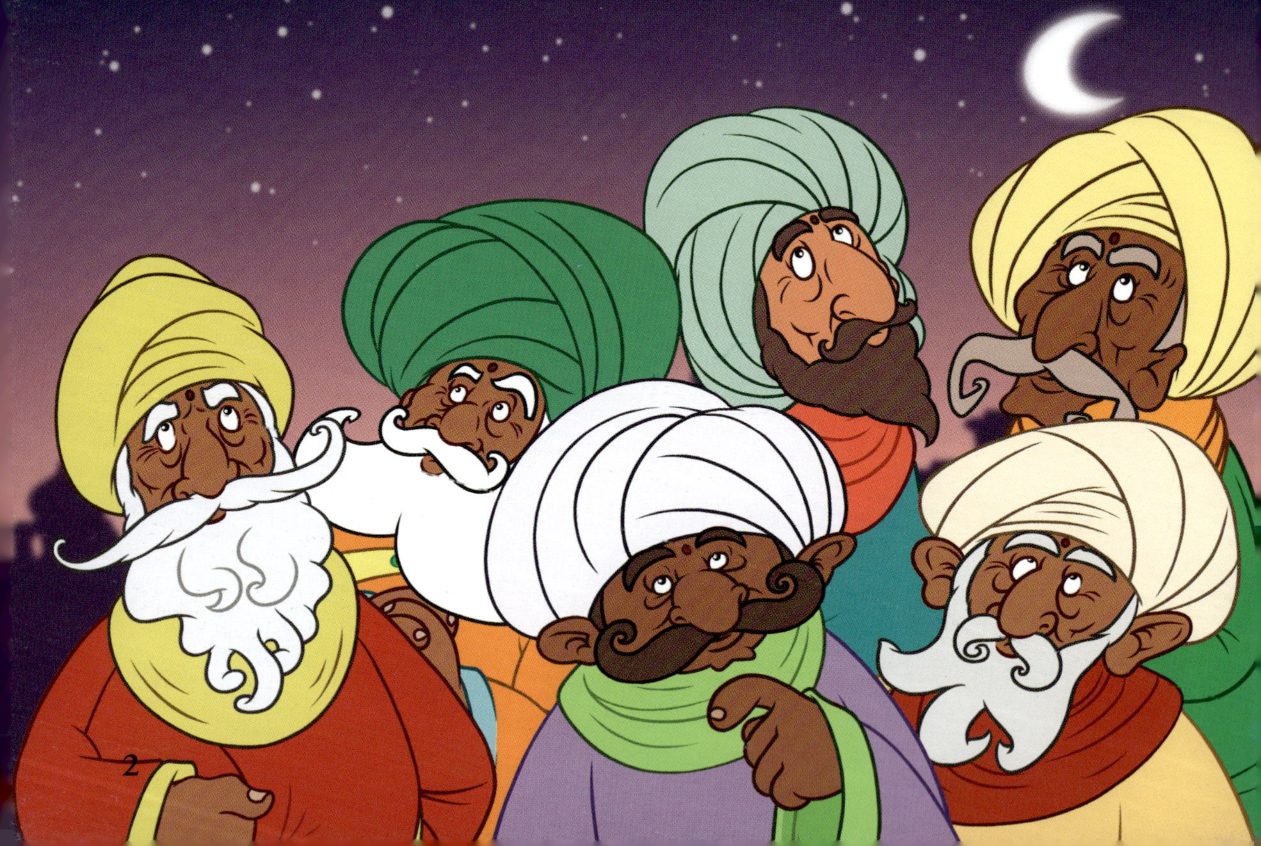

However it hadn't made them wise. Instead all that gazing at the sun and the moon and the stars had hurt their eyes. In fact they had all become blind – which just goes to show how silly they really were!

One day an elephant came to the town. None of the
Six Wisest Men in the Whole World had ever seen an
elephant before. They asked a little boy to take them
close to the elephant.

"We want to see what this animal looks like," they said.

"But you are blind!" said the little boy.

"Yes, but we can feel with our hands, and because we are so wise, we will know what it looks like," said the Six Wisest Men in the Whole World.

Chapter 2

What Does the Elephant Look Like?

The boy took them to the elephant.

The first Wise Man put out his hands to feel the elephant, and he touched the elephant's side. "Goodness me!" said the first Wise Man. "This animal is like a strong brick *wall*!"

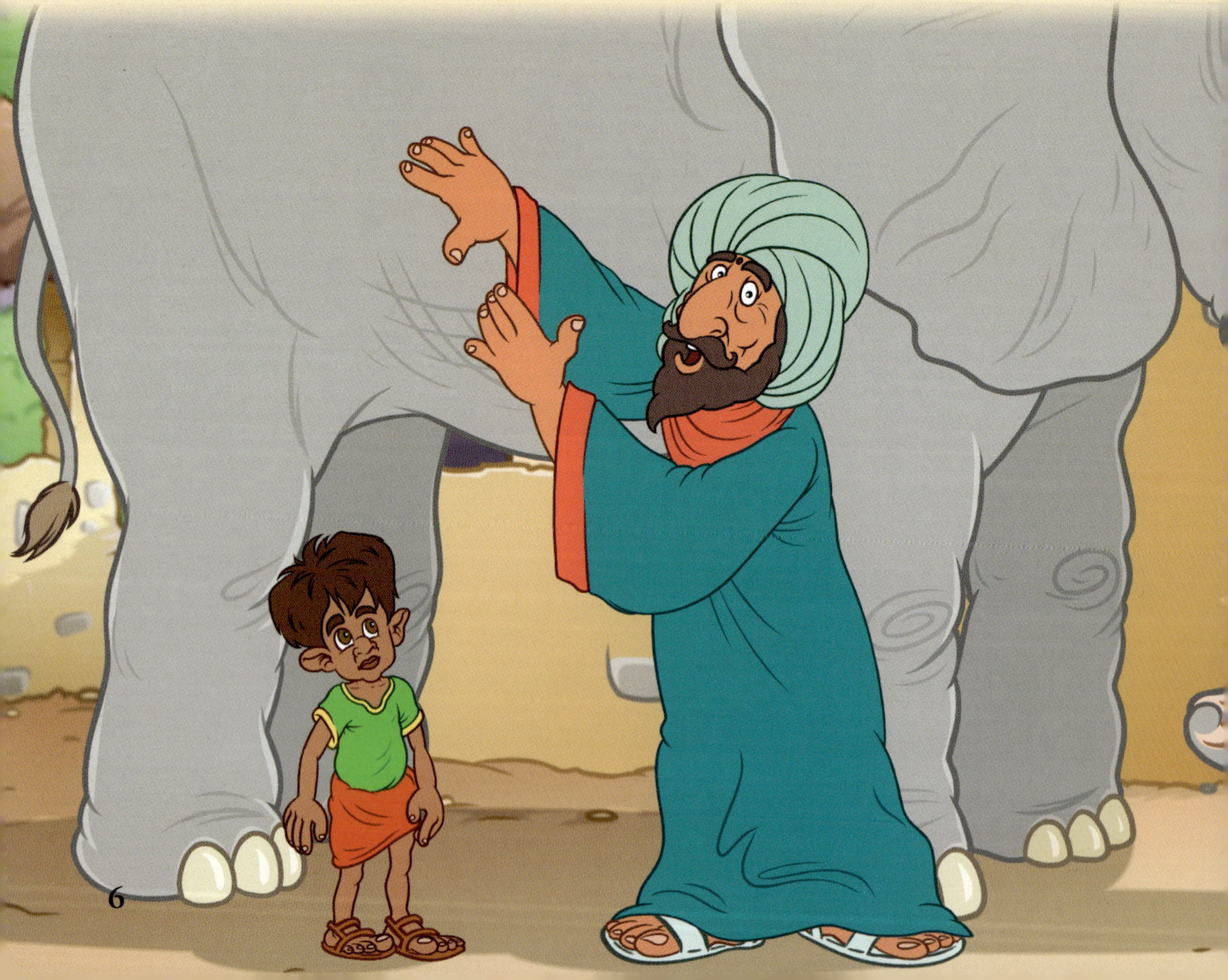

"That can't be right," said the second Wise Man. He put out his hands to feel the elephant, and he ran them over the elephant's sharp tusk. "Goodness me!" he said. "This animal is like a dangerous *spear*!"

"That can't be right," said the third Wise Man, and he put out his hands to feel the elephant. He touched the elephant's trunk and then wrapped his hands around it. He nodded his head. "You are all wrong!" said the third Wise Man. "This animal is like a slithery *snake*!"

"That can't be right," said the fourth Wise Man, and he put out his hands to feel the elephant. Now he happened to touch the elephant's leg. He ran his hands around it and laughed. "How silly you all are!" he said. "This animal is like an enormous *tree*!"

"That can't be right," said the fifth Wise Man, and he put out his hands to feel the elephant. What he touched was the elephant's ear. He gave it a good tug and then turned to the others. "You call yourselves wise men?" he said. "This animal is not like any of these things. This animal is like a fluttery *fan*!"

"A fan?" said the sixth Wise Man. "Let me feel," and he put out his hand. Now he happened to be standing at the back of the elephant, and what he took hold of was the elephant's tail. "What nonsense!" said the sixth Wise Man. "This animal twists and twirls like a piece of *rope*!"

The Six Wisest Men in the Whole World began to argue with each other.

13

Chapter 3

What Is This Animal Really Like?

Finally the Six Wisest Men in the Whole World turned to the boy.

"Tell us, little boy," they said. "What is this animal really like?"

"Well," said the boy, giving the elephant a bucket of water. "It's really like a *fountain*."

"A *fountain*?" said the Six Wisest Men in the Whole World, and they scratched their heads.

Just then the elephant put its trunk into the bucket and sucked up all the water.

Then it lifted its trunk in the air . . .
and showered the water all over the Six Wisest Men in the Whole World!

The Six Wisest Men in the Whole World were amazed.

"You're right!" they said. "So now we know what an elephant is really like. It's like a fountain!" Then they all went home together feeling much happier.

As for the little boy, he just climbed up on the elephant's back and rode off down the street, laughing as he went.